Drat! You Copycat!

by Nancy Krulik • illustrated by John & Wendy

Grosset & Dunlap

For Mandy and Ian—N.K.

Library of Congress Cataloging-in-Publication Data

Krulik, Nancy E.
  Drat! You copycat! / by Nancy Krulik ; illustrated by John & Wendy.
    p. cm. — (Katie Kazoo, switcheroo ; 7)
Summary: Katie agrees to be a buddy for the new girl in class even though her best friend Suzanne does not approve.
  [1. First day of school—Fiction. 2. Moving, Household—Fiction. 3. Schools—Fiction. 4. Magic—Fiction.] I. John & Wendy, ill. II. Title.
  PZ7.K944Dr 2003
  [Fic]—dc21

                                                                2003005965

                10 9 8 7 6 5 4 3 2 1

Proprietary ISBN 978-1-101-95132-3
Part of Boxed Set, ISBN 978-1-101-95128-6

Chapter 1

"Boys and girls, say hello to Becky Stern," Mrs. Derkman told class 3A .

It was early Monday morning. The teacher was standing in the front of the classroom. Beside her was a small girl with a long, blond ponytail.

"Hi, Becky," the kids all said at once.

"Becky and her family have just moved here from Atlanta. I know you will all try to make her feel welcome," Mrs. Derkman said.

The class stared at Becky. Becky stared back at the class. Her blue eyes were wide open. Her face was pale. She looked really scared.

Katie Carew raised her hand.

"Yes Katie?" Mrs. Derkman replied.

"Who is going to be Becky's buddy?"

Jeremy Fox, one of Katie's best friends, smiled proudly when Katie said that. It had been his idea to give new students a buddy when they started at school. That way they'd have a friend right away.

"Well, Katie," Mrs. Derkman said, "would you like to be Becky's buddy?"

Katie grinned. "Sure."

"Becky, stick with Katie this week. She'll show you around. Now take a seat at the empty desk in the second row." Mrs. Derkman said.

All eyes were on Becky as she sat down.

"Okay, everyone," Mrs. Derkman announced. "Please pull out your vocabulary notebooks and copy down this week's word list."

As Katie opened her notebook, a tightly folded piece of paper landed on her desk. She hoped Mrs. Derkman hadn't seen that.

Mrs. Derkman hated it when kids passed notes. Sometimes she even read the notes out loud. That could be very embarrassing.

But right now, Mrs. Derkman had her back turned to the class. She hadn't seen a thing. *Phew.* Katie quickly unfolded the paper.

The note was from Suzanne. "Why did you say you would be her buddy? We were supposed to play double dutch with Miriam and Zoe today. The new girl is wearing a

dress. She can't jump rope in a dress. All the boys will see her underpants."

Katie wasn't sure what to write back. Suzanne's note was kind of mean. It wasn't like Katie had been trying to ruin Suzanne's recess. She was just trying to help the new girl.

But Suzanne was one of Katie's best friends. Katie didn't want her to be mad. She quickly scribbled back an answer. "Becky's new. I was just trying to be nice. Maybe we can all do something else instead."

Just then, Mrs. Derkman turned to face the class. Katie quickly shoved the paper into her desk.

"Okay, class, our first vocabulary word is *bauble*," Mrs. Derkman said. "Can anyone use it in a sentence?"

"I got one," George Brennan shouted out from his seat in the front row. "When I really stink, I take a *bauble* bath!"

Everyone started laughing—everyone

except Mrs. Derkman, anyway.

Mrs. Derkman shook her head. "George, that's not how we behave in class. I don't want to have to talk to you again," she warned sternly. The teacher turned to the rest of the class. "A bauble is a small trinket. Now, does anyone else have a sentence?"

Suzanne raised her hand high.

"Yes, Suzanne," Mrs. Derkman said.

Suzanne sat up straight and smiled as everyone looked at her. "To a princess, an emerald necklace is just a bauble," she said.

Katie choked back a laugh. Somehow, Suzanne always found a way to talk about jewelry, makeup, or fashion.

"Very nice, Suzanne," Mrs. Derkman said. "Anyone else have a sentence?"

Becky shyly raised her hand.

"Okay, Becky," Mrs. Derkman said.

"To Queen Elizabeth, a diamond ring is just a bauble," Becky said in her slow, Southern accent.

"That's just like what you said," Kevin whispered to Suzanne.

Suzanne didn't answer him. She just stared at her own bauble—a plastic diamond ring she wore on her finger.

Katie didn't like vocabulary very much. She liked reading and history a lot more.

Before she knew it, her notebook page was filled with all sorts of doodles. Katie always drew when she got bored.

It seemed like forever until Mrs. Derkman looked at the clock that hung over the classroom doorway. "It's time for lunch," she said finally. "Let's line up."

"All right!" shouted Kevin. "Tomato time!"

"What's he talking about?" Becky asked softly, as she walked over to where Katie and Suzanne were standing.

Katie grinned. "You'll see," she said. "Lunchtime is always tomato time for Kevin."

Becky forced a nervous smile to her lips. "Thanks for saying you'd be my buddy this week," she said in her thick Southern accent. "I hope I'm not getting in the way of anything y'all wanted to do."

Suzanne glanced over at the two double-Dutch jump ropes Miriam was carrying down to the lunchroom for recess. "Well, as a matter of fact . . ." she began.

But Katie didn't let Suzanne finish. She knew whatever Suzanne said would hurt Becky's feelings. Suzanne sometimes said mean things. It wasn't that Suzanne wasn't nice. She just didn't always think before she spoke.

Becky hadn't had a chance to see Suzanne's good side—the side of her that was fun and exciting, and made you feel important just because you were her friend. Katie wanted Becky to know that Suzanne was really a good person.

"She's just kidding," Katie assured Becky. "We can all play together. Suzanne's great at coming up with fun stuff to do."

Suzanne glared at Katie.

Katie ignored her.

"Come on," Katie urged Becky. "Let's go to the cafeteria. I want to get there before all the chocolate pudding is gone."

Chapter 2

Katie showed Becky where the lunch line was in the cafeteria. She helped her get a tray and pick out her food.

Once the girls paid for their lunches, they carried their trays over to a table near the windows. Suzanne was already sitting there with Miriam Chan, Mandy Banks, and some of the other kids in class 3A .

Becky took a seat beside Katie. She smiled at Suzanne. Suzanne barely even glanced in Becky's direction. Instead she opened her pink and purple lunch bag. Inside was a small plastic container. Suzanne tore off the lid and showed everyone a strange-looking mix of

rice, lentil beans, and tomato sauce.

Manny Gonzalez looked across the table at Suzanne's lunch. "Ooh! Gross!" he shouted. He made a grunting noise. "I think I'm gonna puke!"

Suzanne rolled her eyes. "That shows what you know. This is *kosheri*. It's a recipe from Egypt. I'll bet Cleopatra ate it."

"Oh no, here we go again," Manny moaned.

Becky looked curiously at Katie.

"Suzanne is crazy about Cleopatra," Katie explained to her.

"It's all she's talked about for the past two weeks," Manny said.

"That's better than last month, when all she talked about was that artist, Vincent van Gogh," Mandy told Becky.

"She kept telling us how he chopped his ear off," Katie said. "Yuck."

"You're lucky. Hearing about Cleopatra's better than that," Mandy assured Becky.

"Cleopatra was better than anyone," Suzanne insisted. "She was the most powerful woman in ancient Egypt. She was . . ."

"The Queen of the Nile," Katie, Miriam, Mandy, and Manny all finished her sentence for her. They'd heard Suzanne give the same Cleopatra speech about a gazillion times in the past two weeks.

"Well, I don't care who ate that stuff. It's gross," Manny said. "It looks like something George would do with his food."

Katie looked over at George. He'd already begun mixing his spaghetti into his chocolate pudding. George always made a mess of his food. Then he'd wait for someone to dare him to eat it—which he always did.

George cracked Katie up. He told the best jokes. Nothing was too wild or too weird for him to try.

George had also been the one to give Katie her nickname, Katie Kazoo. It sounded a lot like Katie Carew, only cooler. Katie loved it!

Just then, Kevin and Jeremy came over to the table. Kevin's tray was stacked high with tomatoes—round cherry tomatoes, small grape tomatoes, and thick, beefy tomato slices.

"Okay guys, it's tomato time!" Kevin announced happily.

Everyone watched as Jeremy threw one of Kevin's cherry tomatoes up in the air. Kevin opened his mouth wide—and caught it easily. Some of the kids clapped. Kevin took a bow and chomped away.

"Kevin's going for the world record," Katie

explained to Becky. "He's already eaten two hundred thirty-seven tomatoes this month!"

"I love tomatoes," Becky interrupted. She smiled at Kevin. "One time I ate a tomato this big." She held her arms in a circle the size of a pumpkin.

Kevin rolled his eyes. "Tomatoes don't grow that big," he told her, "not even prize-winning ones. You can't fool me. I know all about tomatoes. I've read books on them and everything."

Becky blushed tomato red.

Suzanne didn't want to discuss tomatoes. She wasn't finished talking about Cleopatra.

"You know, I asked my mother to get me a cat," she told the other girls.

"Did she say yes?" Katie asked excitedly. "It's so great having a pet. You know how much fun Pepper and I have together." Pepper was Katie's chocolate-brown-and-white cocker spaniel. She adored him.

"Well a cat is different than a dog," Suzanne said. "I mean, dogs are fun and all, but cats are smart. The ancient Egyptians worshipped them—even Cleopatra."

"*Pepper's* smart," Katie insisted. "I taught him a new trick the other day. When I hold up a treat, he dances on his hind legs."

"Pepper *is* smart," Suzanne assured her best friend. "For a dog, anyway," she added under her breath.

"I used to have a dog," Becky told Katie. She turned to Suzanne. "But now I have a cat.

Her name's Fluffy. She's white and cuddly. And she's *really* smart." She turned to Suzanne and smiled. "Maybe you'll want to come over and play with her one day."

Suzanne ate a forkful of lentil beans.

"Hey Kevin, what do you call a pet tomato?" George asked.

"What?" Kevin asked between bites of a tomato wedge. Red tomato juice dribbled out of his mouth and onto his chin.

"Call it anything you want," George laughed. "It can't hear you!"

Jeremy laughed so hard at George's joke that milk came out of his nose.

George smiled. "Jeremy, you're the best audience. You'll laugh at anything."

Becky looked at Jeremy and smiled. "I know a good joke," she told him.

Suzanne rolled her eyes. "I'm finished eating," she said, before Becky could tell her joke. "Let's go play double Dutch."

"I love double Dutch," Becky said. "Back

in Atlanta we used to have contests to see who could jump the longest without missing. I was always the winner."

Miriam, Mandy, and Zoe Canter were impressed.

Suzanne wasn't. She turned to Becky. "I'd ask you to play, but you're wearing a dress . . . unless you've got shorts under there."

Becky shook her head. "I never thought to do that."

"All the girls in our class wear shorts underneath their dresses," Zoe told her. "That way you can play and no one sees your underpants."

"Wow!" Becky exclaimed.

"It was Suzanne's idea," Miriam said.

"Suzanne is definitely the fashion expert around here," Katie agreed.

Suzanne laughed. "Everyone needs a hobby."

Becky looked at Suzanne's leopard-print shirt. It had fake fur on the cuffs. Her pants were glittery-black.

Katie had hoped Suzanne would have wanted to do something else at recess. But it was clear that wasn't going to happen. Sometimes Suzanne could be so stubborn.

But Katie didn't want to argue with her in front of everyone. That would just make Becky feel bad. "You guys go ahead and jump rope," she told the others, finally. "Becky and I can do something else. Maybe play foursquare."

"It's okay, Katie," Becky said. "If you want to jump rope, I can just watch for today."

"No way," Katie told Becky. "There's always lots of fun stuff going on during recess."

Katie smiled warmly at Becky. But the new girl wasn't looking in Katie's direction. She was busy watching Suzanne's sparkly silver sneakers move back and forth as Suzanne walked away.

Chapter 3

The next morning, Katie was the first kid to arrive at Cherrydale Elementary School. She wanted to be there before Becky arrived. Katie took the job of being Becky's school buddy very seriously.

She sat down on a woooden bench and looked around nervously. It was creepy being the only one on the playground. Everything was so quiet . . . and lonely.

Katie didn't like being alone. Lately it seemed as though whenever she was all by herself, strange things happened.

It had all started a few weeks ago on one really horrible day. Katie had lost the football game for her team. She'd fallen in the mud and ruined her favorite jeans. Then, as if all that weren't bad enough, Katie had burped really loudly in front of the whole class!

The day had been so incredibly, unbelievably awful that Katie had wished she could be anyone but herself. There must have been a shooting star flying overhead or something, because the very next day the magic wind came.

The magic wind was like no wind Katie had seen before. It was a wild, fierce tornado that only blew around Katie.

But the tornado-like gusts weren't the worst part of the magic wind.

The worst part came *after* the wind had stopped blowing. That's when the magic wind turned Katie into someone else.

The magic wind could turn Katie into anyone! One time it transformed her into Suzanne's baby sister, Heather. Suzanne had almost changed Katie's diaper! How

embarrassing would *that* have been?

But even that wasn't as bad as the time the wind turned her into Jeremy Fox. Katie didn't know anything about being a boy!

Katie knew the magic wind wasn't through with her yet. It could show up at any time—as long as no one but Katie was around.

"Hey, Katie Kazoo, you're here early," George called out as he rode his skateboard onto the playground.

Katie was glad someone else had arrived.

"Skateboarding is so cool!" George exclaimed. "That's why I'm doing my research project on the history of skateboarding."

Katie gulped. The research project! Katie had been so excited about being Becky's buddy that she'd forgotten to think of a topic.

"What are you going to research?" George asked her.

"Well, I . . . uh . . ." Katie stammered. Out of the corner of her eye, she spotted the picture frame key chain on her backpack. It had a photo of her dog in it.

"I'm going to do my research project about cocker spaniels," Katie blurted out.

Phew. Pepper didn't know it, but he had just saved Katie.

"That doesn't sound like too *ruff* of a topic," George teased her. "You should be able to find a lot of information *fur* your paper."

"Maybe Mrs. Derkman will let me bring Pepper in as an example," Katie said.

George shook his head. "Are you nuts? Mrs. Derkman doesn't even like having Speedy in the classroom. And he's just a hamster. How do you think she'd feel about a dog?"

Katie nodded. "You're right. I'll bring in some pictures."

Just then, Suzanne wandered onto the playground. It was impossible not to notice her. She was wearing a hot pink glittery rugby shirt. Her capri pants were hot pink and covered in glitter, too.

"New outfit?" Katie asked her.

Suzanne nodded. "Yes! It's so me!"

Katie nodded. "No one likes glitter as much as you do!"

"So, what are you doing for your project?" George interrupted. He didn't want to sit there talking about clothes with two girls.

"Well, I . . ." Suzanne began. But before she could finish her sentence, she saw something terrible heading toward the playground. "Oh, no!" she cried out.

"What is it?" Katie asked.

Suzanne was too upset to speak. She just reached out her hand and pointed.

Katie gasped. It was Becky!

She was wearing a leopard-print shirt with fake fur at the cuffs.

Her pants were glittery-black.

It was the exact same outfit Suzanne had worn yesterday.

No one in class 3A had ever bought one of Suzanne's outfits before. They wouldn't dare.

"This is just horrible!" Suzanne moaned.

Chapter 4

Katie walked quietly into room 3A. She hung up her jacket, dropped her homework in the bin, and sat down at her desk. One second later, a note landed on her desk.

The note was from Suzanne. Katie glanced over at her best friend. She'd been really brave to pass the note just then. Mrs. Derkman hadn't even turned her back to the class.

Obviously Suzanne was so angry at Becky, she didn't care if she caught.

Katie slipped the note under her desk and quietly opened the paper. Suzanne's writing was big, thick, and dark. There were only four words on the paper.

BECKY IS A COPYCAT!

Katie took out her pink pen and scribbled an answer to Suzanne's note.

"Maybe she didn't know you always wear glitter," she wrote.

"Kevin," Katie whispered. "Could you pass this to Suzanne?"

Kevin sat, right between Katie and Suzanne. "I'm not getting in trouble," he said.

Katie sighed. It was too dangerous for her to throw the note to Suzanne. If Mrs. Derkman read this note out loud, Becky's feelings would be hurt.

"I'll give you my dessert at lunch if you'll pass the note," she whispered quickly.

Kevin thought for a moment. "And the tomatoes from your salad, too?" he asked.

Katie nodded.

Kevin quickly snatched the note from Katie's hand and slipped it to Suzanne.

Katie watched as Suzanne unfolded the paper. Suzanne frowned, and shook her head.

"Whose side are you on?" she hissed over Kevin's head.

"I'm not on anyone's side," Katie whispered back.

"Girls!" Mrs. Derkman said sternly. "Is there something you want to share with the entire class?"

For one scary moment, Katie thought Suzanne might call Becky a copycat in front everyone. But Suzanne didn't say anything. She just sat up tall and glared at the back of Becky's head.

"Okay then," Mrs. Derkman said. "Let's get to work. The first thing I want to discuss are your topics for your research papers." "Let's begin with the first row."

George sat in the first seat in the first row. Mrs. Derkman had put him there so she could keep an eye on him. "I'm doing a paper on skateboarding," George told her. "It will be *wheel-y* exciting."

A few of the kids groaned at George's bad joke. Mrs. Derkman never even looked up. She just wrote George's topic in her notebook. "Okay, how about you, Mandy?"

"I want to do a research paper on dragon-flies. We have a lot of them living near the creek behind my house," Mandy answered.

"That will be very nice," Mrs. Derkman said. "Just please don't bring any of them into the classroom."

Everybody laughed. They all knew that Mrs. Derkman was very afraid of bugs.

"And you, Jeremy?" Mrs. Derkman asked.

"I want to do a report on soccer," Jeremy said. "It's my favorite sport."

"Just remember, you can't play ball in the classroom," Mrs. Derkman reminded him.

"I'm going to make a videotape," Jeremy assured her.

Mrs. Derkman smiled. "That's a fine idea. Okay, now let's move on to the second row. Have you come up with something, Becky?"

Becky sat up very straight and tall. "I want to do my research project on Cleopatra," she said.

The class was silent.

They couldn't believe their ears. Everyone figured Suzanne would be the one to do a research project about Cleopatra. The kids all turned around to see how Suzanne was taking the news: *not* well.

Suzanne's eyes were closed in angry little slits. Her mouth was clenched tightly. She was obviously really mad—so mad, in fact, that she forgot Mrs. Derkman's rule about calling out.

"That's my topic!" Suzanne shouted. "I was going to do Cleopatra! Everybody knew it."

Becky shook her head. "I didn't know it."

Suzanne glared at her. "Yes you did. You knew how I felt about Cleopatra. You heard

me talking about her at lunch. Becky, you're a great big copycat!"

The class gasped. No one had ever acted that way in Mrs. Derkman's room before. Not even George.

"Suzanne Lock," Mrs. Derkman said sternly. "That is *not* how we behave in class. Becky will be doing a report on Cleopatra. You will have to find another topic to research. There are lots of interesting people or things you can learn about."

"Not as interesting as Cleopatra," Suzanne moaned.

Mrs. Derkman sighed. "Oh, I think there are. In fact, I'm going to give you a topic for your project. You will do a report on Coco Chanel."

"What's a Coco Chanel?" Suzanne demanded. "Some sort of candy bar?"

Mrs. Derkman laughed. "No. Coco Chanel was a person. A very special person."

"Why?" Suzanne asked.

"You'll see," Mrs. Derkman said, as she wrote the topic in her book. She smiled at Suzanne. "I promise that you—of all people—will find her very interesting."

Suzanne sat back, folded her arms, and stared furiously at Becky.

Katie gulped. She'd seen that look on Suzanne's face before. *I'm sure glad I'm not Becky,* she thought to herself.

Chapter 5

"Now do you believe me? I told you Becky was a copycat!" Suzanne insisted, as she and Katie walked out of the school building at the end of the day.

Katie nodded slowly. She couldn't defend Becky anymore. Taking Suzanne's research topic had been really mean.

"I can't believe Mrs. Derkman is making me do a research project on that Coco Chanel person," Suzanne moaned. "I don't even know who she is."

"You can come over to my house and we can look her up on the Internet," Katie suggested.

Suzanne shrugged. "Why not? At least I'll

be able to eat some of your mom's cookies while we work."

Katie grinned. Her mom did bake great cookies. Suzanne's mother usually served the store-bought kind.

Just then, Becky came running up to the girls. "Are y'all going to the library to start

your research?" she asked in her soft Southern accent.

Katie was about to tell Becky that she and Suzanne were going to her house to use the computer, but Suzanne shot Katie one of her don't-you-dare looks.

Becky looked hopefully at Katie. That made Katie feel terrible. She was supposed to be Becky's buddy, and she wasn't inviting her to come along. Katie knew Becky was feeling left out.

But Suzanne's feelings had been hurt, too. She needed Katie every bit as much as Becky did. Katie didn't know what to do.

Suzanne solved that problem for her.

"We have other plans," Suzanne told Becky simply. "You'll have to float down the Nile without us."

Becky looked curiously at Suzanne.

"The Nile," Suzanne repeated. "That's a river in Egypt. You'd have known that if you were as big a fan of Cleopatra as I am."

Becky smiled. "I'm going to learn all about Cleopatra. Then you and I can talk about her. Maybe we can even start a Cleopatra club."

"Whatever." Suzanne sighed. She put her thumbs together and held her pointer fingers straight up to make a big W.

This was going to get ugly—Katie could tell. She quickly grabbed Suzanne by the elbow. "We've got to go. See you tomorrow, Becky."

"I don't believe that girl!" Suzanne exclaimed, as she and Katie walked off. "A Cleopatra club? How could she?"

"She just wants to be friends." Katie said.

Suzanne rolled her eyes. "I'd rather be friends with a three-headed rat."

Katie sighed. There was no point in arguing with Suzanne when she was this angry. It was easier to change the topic. "You can use the Internet first," she told her. "I have a book on cocker spaniels that I can start with."

Before long, the girls had reached Katie's

house. Mrs. Carew was sitting on the front steps with Pepper when they arrived.

"Hi, girls," she greeted them. "How was school?"

"Rotten," Suzanne moaned.

"Fine," Katie said at the exact same time.

Mrs. Carew laughed. "Are you sure you were in the same classroom?" She held out a plate of warm sugar cookies with M&M's baked into them.

"The new girl stole my research topic," Suzanne explained between cookie bites. "Katie got the topic she wanted."

"Cocker spaniels," Katie told her mother.

Mrs. Carew laughed as Katie scratched Pepper behind the ears. "Of course," she said.

"I wanted to do Cleopatra. But Blechy Becky is researching her," Suzanne said. "Mrs. Derkman is making me do a report on some lady named Coco Chanel."

"Oh, you're going to love Coco!" Katie's mom exclaimed. "She's very interesting."

Suzanne made a face.

"Besides, you already know everything there is to know about Cleopatra," Mrs. Carew said. "Now you'll learn something new."

Katie and Suzanne looked at each other. That was one of those things only a grown-up would say. You couldn't argue with it—even though you wished you could.

"Let's go find out who this Coco Chanel lady is," Katie told Suzanne.

Suzanne nodded and followed Katie into the living room. The girls sat down and booted up the computer. Suzanne typed the words

"Coco Chanel" into the search engine. Almost instantly the link to a short biography appeared on the screen.

Coco Chanel: This French fashion designer's real name was Gabrielle Chanel. Coco Chanel changed fashion forever. She designed the first pants for women. She was famous for wearing lots of beads and carrying quilted pocketbooks with chains. She also created perfumes.

"Oooh! Katie, look at her," Suzanne squealed, pointing to the photograph.

Katie looked at the picture of a dark-haired woman in a black pantsuit. She wore strands and strands of white pearls around her neck. She looked very elegant.

"Isn't she wonderful?" Suzanne asked Katie. "Don't you just love all those beads? Do you think I should wear my hair short like that?"

Katie laughed. Good-bye Cleo, Hello Coco.

Chapter 6

"Teddy bear, teddy bear, turn around. Teddy bear, teddy bear, touch the ground," Becky chanted as she jumped over the two double-Dutch jump ropes.

Becky, Miriam, and Zoe were already playing in the schoolyard when Katie arrived the next morning. Katie walked over to watch.

"Teddy bear, teddy bear, touch your toe," Becky continued as she tapped her foot with her hand. "Teddy bear, teddy bear, out you go!" she shouted as she dashed out from between the twirling ropes.

"That was great!" Miriam congratulated Becky. "You didn't miss once."

Becky smiled and looked over at Katie. "Hi! Where's Suzanne?"

Katie shrugged. "We don't usually walk to school together. Why?" After what had happened yesterday, Katie couldn't believe that Becky would be looking for Suzanne.

"I just thought she'd like to jump double Dutch with me. I know a whole bunch of jump-rope rhymes."

Katie didn't think Suzanne would want to learn any of Becky's rhymes, but she didn't tell Becky that. Instead, she said, "Nice outfit. Is it new?"

Becky was wearing a purple shirt with a pink flower in the center. The shirt matched her purple glittery skirt perfectly.

"I found it at the mall," Becky told her. "I thought it was really cool." She lifted her skirt a little. "And see, I'm wearing shorts."

"Do you want to jump again, Becky?" Zoe interrupted. "Since you didn't miss, you get another turn."

"Okay," Becky said. As Miriam and Zoe
began turning the ropes, Becky leaped in.
"Fortune-teller if you're so smart, tell me the
name of my sweetheart. Is it A . . . B . . . C . . ."

Becky kept jumping, twirling around as
she said each letter. The ropes were moving at
a very steady rhythm, until suddenly . . .

"Look at Suzanne!" Zoe cried out. She
dropped one of her ropes. Instantly, Becky

tripped over the fallen jump rope. "Hey! Why did you stop turning?" she asked.

But there was no one around to answer her. Miriam and Zoe were both running over to meet Suzanne at the far end of the playground.

"Wow, Suzanne! You look great," Mandy Banks exclaimed. "I love those beads."

Suzanne fingered the many strands of white plastic beads she wore around her neck. She smoothed the creases in her black slacks and straightened her plain black shirt.

Katie was amazed. The girls had only seen the picture of Coco Chanel yesterday. And Suzanne was already dressed like her.

"Hey there, Coco," Katie teased.

"Don't you just love this outfit?" Suzanne gushed. "My mom helped me put it together. She's so glad that I'm over all that glitter stuff." Suzanne stared at Becky's outfit.

Just then George and Jeremy wandered over to see what all the fuss was about.

"What are you supposed to be?" Jeremy asked.

"Let me check my calendar," George said. "I think I missed Halloween."

Suzanne rolled her eyes. "You boys don't know anything. This outfit is very grown-up."

"But you're not a grown-up, Suzanne," Jeremy reminded her. "How are you going to play any games in that getup?"

"Maybe I don't feel like playing games," Suzanne argued.

"What are you going to do at recess then?"

"I'm going to spend recess drawing clothes," she told him.

George made a face. "Boring!" he said.

"No, it's not!" Suzanne replied. "I can get lots of ideas for new fashions here. As Coco Chanel said, 'Fashion is in the air. Born upon the wind.' "

George and Jeremy had no idea what Suzanne was talking about.

"Forget Coco Chanel," George moaned.

"You're *Cuckoo* Chanel."

Jeremy laughed. "See ya later, Cuckoo," he said as he ran off toward the soccer field.

"Cuckoo, cuckoo," George added, sounding very much like a cuckoo clock.

As soon as the boys were gone, Becky held up a her purple lunch bag. "I brought lunch today," she told Suzanne. "It's pita bread and bean salad. I've got dried figs for dessert. I thought we could share our lunches and have an Egyptian feast."

Suzanne shook her head. "Sorry, Becky. I have French bread and a hunk of cheese for lunch today. That's what they eat in Paris. Coco Chanel lived in Paris, you know."

Becky bit her lip. "Oh. Well, bread and cheese sounds good, too."

"It is," Suzanne assured her. "I love every- thing that's French. As far as I'm concerned, Egypt is ancient history!"

Chapter 7

"Look at Blechy Becky," Suzanne said as she watched Becky drag a huge black duffel bag to her desk. It had been two weeks since Becky had chosen Cleopatra as her research topic, but Suzanne still didn't like her.

"What do you think she has in there?" Mandy wondered.

"Maybe a mummy," Suzanne joked. "That would be perfect. After all, only a *dead person* would hang around with her."

"That's really mean, Suzanne," Katie said.

"Not as mean as copying my clothes and stealing my research topic," Suzanne said.

"She's probably got the stuff for her report

in that bag," Katie said.

Today was the first day of the research project presentations. Two kids would give speeches each day. George and Becky were first.

"She sure doesn't look like Cleopatra," Suzanne said, staring at Becky's white blouse, black stretch jeans, and chunky red beads. "The Queen of the Nile didn't wear beads. Coco Chanel wore beads. *I* wear beads. She's not trying to be like Cleopatra. She's trying to be like me. She's such a wanna-be."

Before Katie could say a word, Mrs. Derkman stood in front of the room. "Will everyone sit down, please?" she said.

The kids quickly scrambled to their seats.

"We're going to get started on our research presentations," the teacher continued. "George, do you want to go first?"

Katie glanced over at George. He was wearing baggy orange shorts and a huge yellow-and-orange Hawaiian shirt. He was

also wearing his helmet and pads. He
certainly looked ready to go first.

"Sure!" George exclaimed. He walked to
the front of the room and held up his skateboard. "Hey there, dudes and honeys. This is
my stick."

Mrs. Derkman looked curiously at George.
"Excuse me?"

George laughed. "All I said was, 'Hi everyone. This is my board.' I was using surfing
slang."

"I thought your report was about skateboarding," Manny interrupted.

"It is," George said. "Skateboarding
became really popular in the 1950s. Back
then, everyone in California was surfing.
Other kids wanted to surf, too. But not everyone lived near an ocean. So skateboards were
great. You could catch the surfing wave no
matter where you lived. That's why a lot of
skateboarding words sound like surfer words."

George put one foot on the back of his

skateboard. "I'm going to show you a cool skateboarding move," he told the class. "It's called Mondo Foot."

Mondo foot? Katie couldn't help it. She started to giggle. So did lots of other kids.

"No, really," George told them. "When you do Mondo Foot, you push the board with your front foot, like this."

George pushed off with his front foot. His skateboard soared across the floor.

Unfortunately, George wasn't on the skateboard. He'd slipped off. *Crash!* The board slammed into the trash can. Trash spilled out all over the floor.

George leaped across the room to grab his board. As he ran, he tripped over the fallen trash can. George went flying through the air. He landed headfirst right on top of Katie's desk.

George was lucky he was wearing a helmet.

Too bad Katie wasn't. George slammed right into her face.

"Ouch!" Katie shouted, as she grabbed her nose.

"I'm sorry," George mumbled. He looked embarrassed.

"It's okay," Katie told him. "I'm alright."

But Katie *wasn't* alright. Her nose was bleeding.

"Oooh! Yuck!" Kevin shouted when he saw the red blood running from Katie's nose. He moved his chair far from Katie.

Mrs. Derkman walked over and handed Katie a wad of tissues. "It's just a little blood,

Kevin," she said. "Katie, go to the nurse and get an ice pack. George, finish your report without any more demonstrations, alright?"

"Okay," George said. He sounded disappointed.

Katie held the tissues tightly against her nose as she headed out of the room and down the long, empty hallway to the nurse's office. She was determined not to get any blood on her shirt.

Suddenly, Katie felt a cool wind blowing on the back of her neck. She quickly looked around. There were no windows in the hallway, and the doors were all shut tight.

Katie gulped. This was no ordinary wind. This was the magic wind!

The magic wind began spinning faster and faster all around Katie. Her red hair whipped wildly around her head.

Katie shut her eyes tightly, and tried not to cry. As the fierce tornado swirled, she grabbed onto a locker.

And then it stopped. Just like that. No
warning. But Katie wasn't surprised. The
magic wind never gave her any warning. In
fact, it never felt the same way twice. The
magic wind was always different—as different
as the people it turned Katie into.

Which brought up the big question: Just
who had the magic wind turned Katie into
this time?

Chapter 8

Katie was afraid to open her eyes. She had no idea where she was. All she knew was that she was sitting, and she used to be standing.

Suddenly, Katie heard loud applause. Where was she? A theater? A ball game?

Slowly, Katie let her eyes flutter open.

"Oh my goodness," she muttered to herself. "How did I wind up here?"

Somehow, Katie had come back to class 3A. Everyone was sitting happily in their seats. George was standing in the front of the room, taking a bow.

"That was very good, George," Mrs. Derkman said, as she walked to the front of the room. "We have all learned a lot about skateboarding."

"And about skate*falling*," Manny teased.

George blushed.

"Okay, please take your seat, George," Mrs. Derkman said. "Now we will hear all about Cleopatra. It's your turn, Becky."

Suddenly, all eyes turned to look at Katie. Katie stared back at her classmates.

"Becky?" Mrs. Derkman said. She walked over to where Katie was sitting.

Slowly, Katie looked down. Instead of her own faded jeans and blue shirt, Katie was wearing a white blouse, black stretch jeans, and big red beads.

Katie gulped as she wiped a strand of blond hair from her eyes. Oh, no! Katie had turned into Becky. Mrs. Derkman expected her to give a report, but Katie didn't know anything about Cleopatra.

"Becky, it's your turn," Mrs. Derkman coaxed sternly.

Katie didn't know what to do. If she didn't go up in front of the classroom right now, Becky would get an *F* on her report.

Katie couldn't let *that* happen.

But she couldn't teach the class anything about Cleopatra, either.

Then Katie remembered the black bag Becky had dragged to school that day. It was sitting right at her feet. Maybe there was something in the bag that could help her give the report.

"Okay, Mrs. Derkman," Katie said as she unzipped the bag. Her voice sounded so strange. It had the same soft, singsongy Southern accent as the real Becky's.

Slowly, Katie peered into the bag. The first thing she spotted was a package of note cards.

Phew. Becky had written out her speech on the cards.

Then Katie pulled out a black wig and a huge hat with some sort of snake on the top.

Under that was a long, clingy, white dress. There was a stuffed cat in the bag as well.

Quickly, Katie threw the costume on over Becky's everyday clothes. She picked up the cat and the cards, and walked to the front of the room.

Immediately Suzanne started laughing. "Her crown's on backward," She giggled. "The snake's supposed to go in the front!"

"Suzanne!" Mrs. Derkman warned.

Suzanne stopped her giggling right away.

Katie blushed and turned the crown around. Then she looked at the notecards in her hand. They were very hard to read. Becky did not have neat handwriting.

"Cleopatra was born in Egypt in 69 B.C.," Katie began slowly, as she struggled to understand Becky's notes. "She was famous for her beauty."

Katie looked out at the kids in her class. They seemed interested. Well, at least everyone other than Suzanne seemed interested. Things weren't going too badly. She turned to the next card.

"Cleopatra was the daughter of King . . ."

But before Katie could finish her sentence, she lost her grip on the notecards. The the whole pile slipped from her hands.

"Oops!" Katie exclaimed. Quickly, she bent down to scoop up Becky's cards. As she looked down at the cards, the Cleopatra crown fell from Katie's head. The black wig slipped down over her eyes. Katie could barely see past the long dark hair. And as if that weren't bad enough . . .

Rrrip. Becky's long white dress ripped right up the back. Everyone heard the dress tear.

"Boy, Cleopatra must have been a klutz!" George joked.

"This is too funny!" Suzanne began to giggle. So did a lot of other kids.

Katie could feel her face turning red with embarrassment.

"Class!" Mrs. Derkman scolded. "Show Becky the same respect you would like to be shown during your report."

Mrs. Derkman sounded really angry. Instantly, the class got quiet. They waited for Becky to speak.

But the note cards were all out of order now. Katie had no idea what she was supposed to say next. This report was turning into a disaster!

Katie looked out at her classmates. They were all sitting silently, waiting for her to say something.

Quickly, Katie read whatever was written on the card at the top of her pile. "Cleopatra was absolutely crazy about Caesar," she told the class.

"About who?" Manny asked.

"Caesar," Katie repeated.

"Caesar who?" Manny asked.

Katie had no idea. "Um . . . Caesar . . .

Caesar . . . uh . . . Caesar salad." she blurted out finally.

Everyone began laughing again.

Katie thought she was going to cry.

"I think you mean *Julius* Caesar," Suzanne told her. "He was a famous Roman general. Everyone knows that."

Not everyone, Katie thought miserably.

Suzanne started to giggle again. Soon everyone else was laughing, too.

Katie couldn't take it anymore. She ran out of the classroom in tears.

As she raced down the empty hallway, Katie could hear the kids in room 3A making fun of Becky's speech. She could also hear Mrs. Derkman ordering her to come back.

But Katie wasn't going back into that room.

At least not as long as she was Becky Stern.

Chapter 9

Katie ran into the bathroom to wash her face. She couldn't let anyone see her with blotchy skin and red eyes. It was bad enough that she'd ruined Becky's report. She couldn't let everyone think she was a big crybaby, too.

Katie turned on the cold water and put her hands under the faucet. Right away, she felt a draft blowing on her neck.

Katie looked over at the bathroom windows. They were locked tightly. And the door hadn't opened since Katie had walked into the room. Quickly Katie bent down and peered under the two bathroom stalls. There was no one in either one.

Katie was all alone in the girls bathroom.

The magic wind only came when Katie was alone.

Katie grabbed on to the and held on tightly. She knew what was coming next. That breeze was about to become a tornado!

Sure enough, within seconds, wild winds began to swirl all around Katie. This time, the wind was bitter and cold. Katie could feel goosebumps popping up all over her body as the gusts churned around her.

And then it was all over. Just like that. The air was still, and the bathroom was warm again.

Nervously, Katie looked into the bathroom mirror. Her own face stared back at her. She could see her own red hair and the freckles across her nose. Katie Kazoo was back!

And so was Becky. In fact, she was standing right next to Katie, wearing a crooked wig and a ripped white dress, looking confused.

"How did I get in here?" she asked Katie.

"Don't you remember?" Katie replied.

"Well, sort of. I think I was giving my report, but I'm not sure. It's all kind of fuzzy."

Katie gulped. How was she going to explain this? She couldn't just come out and say that she had turned into Becky and given her report for her. Becky would never believe her. Katie wouldn't have believed it, either—if it hadn't happened to her.

"My report was a real mess," Becky moaned. "I'm not sure what happened. It's like it was me up there in front of everyone, but it wasn't me. You know what I mean?"

Katie definitely knew what she meant— better than anyone. "Maybe Mrs. Derkman will let you try again," Katie suggested.

"Do you really think so?" Becky asked.

Katie wasn't sure if Mrs. Derkman would give Becky another chance, but it was worth a try. "You're new," Katie told her. "Tell her you got nervous."

"I *was* kind of nervous, waiting for my turn," Becky recalled.

"And maybe you should volunteer to do a different topic," Katie continued. "Then you're doing extra work."

Becky made a face. "Why would I want to do that? I did so much work on my report."

"Yeah, but you already . . ."

Katie was about to say that Becky had already messed up her Cleopatra report, but that wasn't true. Katie had messed it up for her. So instead she said, "Mrs. Derkman likes when kids do extra work. And you want Mrs. Derkman to like you. It's horrible when she's mad at you. Just ask George. She's always angry with him."

"I guess," Becky said thoughtfully. "What topic should I pick?"

"I don't know. Something you're interested in." She stopped for a minute. "You weren't really all that into Cleopatra, were you?"

Becky looked down at the tile floor. "No."

"Then why did you pick that topic?" Katie asked her.

Becky frowned. "I guess Suzanne made it sound so interesting. She makes everything sound interesting."

Katie nodded. "I know what you mean."

"I thought if Suzanne and I had something in common, we'd be friends. And if Suzanne became my friend, then everyone would be my friend," Becky explained.

"Well, a lot of people do like Suzanne," Katie agreed. "But you don't have to be just like her to make friends. Just be yourself."

"But everyone here is so different than the

kids at my old school. Y'all have been friends forever."

Katie shook her head. "Not all of us. George was new at the beginning of the year. He has lots of friends now. You will, too. It just takes time." She smiled. "I'm your friend, so you've got one pal already."

Becky smiled. "Okay, pal," she said sweetly. "Can you help me come up with a report topic?

"Sure! What do you like to do?" said Katie.

Becky thought about that for a minute. "Well, back in Atlanta I took gymnastics. I was getting pretty good at the balance beam and floor exercises."

"So ask Mrs. Derkman if you can do a report on gymnastics," Katie suggested. Then she frowned and touched her nose. It was still sore where George had crashed into her. "Just don't do a cartwheel into my face, okay?"

Becky giggled and stuck out her hand. "It's a deal."

Chapter 10

"Coco Chanel was known for her simple dresses and suits," Suzanne told the class Thursday morning. "She also created costume jewelry and quilted handbags."

"P.U. What's that smell?" George held his nose and looked all around the room. "I think it's coming from *you*, Suzanne."

Suzanne rolled her eyes. "That's perfume," she told George. "Coco Chanel created all sorts of perfumes. Her most famous is called Chanel Number Five."

"She should have called it *Dog Poo* Number Five," George said. "It smells terrible."

"George!" Mrs. Derkman scolded. "We do

not say 'dog poo' in school."

"Oh, I'm not wearing Chanel perfume," Suzanne said. "I made my perfume myself."

"How did you do that?" Mandy asked.

"I used a perfume-making kit," Suzanne explained. "It's a mixture of bubble gum, grape, and rosebud scents. I call it Suzanne Number One."

Then Suzanne showed the class pictures of clothes that Coco Chanel had designed. The girls seemed interested. The boys were bored.

"Lots of designers copied Coco Chanel's work," Suzanne said, as she finished her report. "Everyone wanted to look like her and dress like her. That's why *I* can relate to her."

Mrs. Derkman stood up and smiled at Suzanne. "I knew this would be a good topic for you to research. Thank you for your report." The teacher turned to Becky. "Are you ready?" she asked her.

Becky stood nervously and straightened the sleeves on her blue and silver gymnastics leotard. She looked at Katie.

Katie smiled and gave her a thumbs-up sign.

Becky gave her a thumbs-up back, then. . .

Whoosh! Becky flipped in midair and landed on her hands! She walked upside down to the front of the room.

Whoosh! Becky flipped over again. This time, she landed on her feet.

"My report is about gymnastics," Becky told them. "People have been doing gymnastics for more than two thousand years. But it's only been a competitive sport for about one hundred years."

Becky gave a long speech about about the history of gymnastics. She didn't use any note cards. She knew it all by heart.

Then Becky demonstrated some of the moves she had learned in her gymnastics classes. She did a back flip, a cartwheel, and a handspring. She ended her routine with a perfect split.

"Awesome!" Jeremy exclaimed.

"I wish I could do that!" George said.

"Can you teach me to do a cartwheel?" Zoe asked. "I always flop over to the side."

Suddenly, everyone was talking at once. They all wanted Becky to teach them how to do gymnastics.

Katie looked at Suzanne. She was playing with her beaded necklace, trying to act as though she didn't like Becky's report. But Katie knew better. It would be impossible not to have found Becky's speech interesting.

"Okay class, settle down," Mrs. Derkman said. "I don't want anyone trying any of Becky's tricks out on the playground. You should only learn gymnastics from a real

gymnastics teacher."

"That's right," Becky said. "My mom found a gymnastics school here in Cherrydale. Maybe some of y'all can take classes there, too."

"Do they have a trampoline?" Miriam said.

"Sure," Becky said.

"How about a vaulting horse?" asked Jeremy.

"Of course."

Becky told the other kids what gymnastics school was like. She didn't seem like a new kid any more. She was one of them now.

There was no reason for Becky to be a copy-cat ever again.

Chapter 11

"This one is called a round-off," Becky said, as she leaped up, flipped, and twisted her body in midair.

"All right, Becky!" Jeremy shouted.

Becky smiled brightly and winked at him. Jeremy blushed.

It was recess. Usually the kids in class 3A would be all over the playground. But today they were all gathered on the grass, watching Becky do her gymnastics. Every time she bent her body or flipped over, they cheered.

Suzanne was the only one in the class not watching Becky. She was sitting all by herself on a bench.

Katie looked over and studied her best friend's face. She looked sad and kind of lonely.

It was weird to see Suzanne like that. Usually Suzanne looked angry, happy, or proud of herself. She never looked sad. And she was *never* alone on the playground. Katie figured the look on Suzanne's face meant trouble for Becky.

And then the strangest thing happened. Becky turned away from the sea of kids surrounding her. She walked over to Suzanne.

"Hi," Becky said shyly.

"What do *you* want?" Suzanne asked.

Becky grinned. "I just wanted to tell you that I thought your report was the best in the whole class. I'd never heard of Coco Chanel before, but now I think she's just the coolest!"

Suzanne smiled . . . a little. "She was pretty cool," she admitted.

"You know what I was thinking?" Becky asked. "You're kind of like the Coco Chanel of our class. You set the fashion trends."

Suzanne's smile broadened. "I was think-ing the same thing." She studied Becky's glittery yellow-and-orange shirt. "Some black beads would look really nice with that," she said.

"You think so?" Becky asked her.

Suzanne nodded. "Coco Chanel wore beads with everything!"

"I don't know where to get beads in Cherrydale," Becky admitted. "I wore my mother's red beads the other day."

"There's a great bead shop at the mall. It's near Katie's mom's bookstore," Suzanne said.

Katie's mom worked part time at the Book Nook bookstore in the Cherrydale Mall.

"Maybe you and I could go and look at beads . . . together," Becky suggested shyly.

"Katie and I are going to the mall Saturday morning. We're going to hand out flyers for her mom's store. You could tag along . . . I guess," Suzanne told her.

Becky shook her head. "I have gymnastics

on Saturday mornings."

"Okay." Suzanne began to walk away.

"But I could meet you later, after my class," Becky said quickly.

"We'll be there until three o'clock," Suzanne told her. "If you come earlier, maybe the three of us could get a slice of pizza at Louie's."

"Is that in the mall, too?"

Suzanne nodded.

"Is it good pizza?" Becky asked.

"The best!" Suzanne said. "Boy, you've got a lot to learn about Cherrydale, Becky."

"I'll see you Saturday," Becky assured her. Then she turned and walked back toward the kids on the grass.

Katie made her way across the playground to Suzanne. "What was that all about?"

"Nothing," Suzanne shrugged. "I just told Becky to meet us at the mall on Saturday. That's all. No biggie."

Katie looked surprised. "So you're friends?" she asked.

Suzanne shrugged. "I don't know about friends . . ." she began. "She's okay, I guess."

"Yeah, Becky's pretty okay," Katie agreed.

"You know, I was thinking," Suzanne continued, "I like dressing like Coco Chanel because she was so cool, smart, and creative. Maybe that's the reason Becky has been acting the way she has. She wants to be like me. Who wouldn't?"

Katie choked back a laugh. Sometimes Suzanne could be so full of herself.

"Besides, Becky's new here," Suzanne continued. "She needs someone with my experience—and flair for fashion—to show her around."

That made Katie angry. She'd been showing Becky around all week. And she'd done a good job of making her feel at home. Katie was about to tell Suzanne just that, when she suddenly felt a cold breeze blowing all around her.

Oh, no! Was the magic wind back? Would it blow with Suzanne standing right there?

"Katie, what's the matter with you?" Suzanne asked. "You look look like you just saw a ghost." Suzanne held her palm up in the air. "I think I just felt a raindrop. And listen to that wind. I think we're going to have a storm."

Katie breathed a sigh of relief. Suzanne could hear the wind, too. This was just a regular storm—the kind everybody could feel.

"I hate rain!" Suzanne moaned.

"The flowers need it. And so do the trees," Katie told her.

Suzanne smiled. "That's why you're my best friend," she said.

"Huh?"

"You're always thinking about someone else," Suzanne explained. "Like the trees. Or Becky. You really wanted to help her."

Katie gulped. *Help her?* Katie had almost ruined everything for her.

But, of course, Suzanne didn't know anything about that.

"I just told her to do a report on something *she* found interesting," Katie said quickly.

Suzanne nodded. "And that report helped her make friends. You knew what she needed. I swear, Katie, sometimes it's like you can get right inside other people's brains."

Katie started to laugh. Inside people's brains? Suzanne didn't know the half of it!

Chapter 12

Did you ever wonder how we know so much about the lives of people in ancient Egypt? Becky found the answer to that question while she was researching Cleopatra. (Of course Suzanne already knew the answer, but that's another story!)

It turns out the ancient Egyptians had a written language. But they didn't use letters in their alphabet. They used pictures. Each picture stood for a sound.

The ancient Egyptians used their picture language to write stories about their lives on the walls of their buildings and pyramids.

At the library, Becky found a chart that

Doggone It!

For the *real* Pepper . . . *AROOOOOO!*

Text copyright © 2003 by Nancy Krulik. Illustrations copyright
© 2003 by John and Wendy. All rights reserved. Published by
Grosset & Dunlap, a division of Penguin Young Readers Group,
345 Hudson Street, New York, NY, 10014. GROSSET & DUNLAP
is a trademark of Penguin Random House LLC.
Manufactured in China

Library of Congress Cataloging-in-Publication Data

Krulik, Nancy E.
  Doggone it! / by Nancy Krulik ; illustrated by John & Wendy.
        p. cm. — (Katie Kazoo, switcheroo ; 8)
Summary: When strict Mrs. Derkman moves next door to third-
grader Katie Carew, scares her friends away, and insists she keep
her dog, Pepper, on a leash, Katie finds a non-magical solution to
the problem. Includes steps for teaching a dog to sit and stay.
  [1. Neighbors—Fiction. 2. Dogs—Fiction. 3. Teachers—Fiction.
4. Magic—Fiction.] I. John & Wendy, ill. II. Title.
  PZ7.K944Dn 2005
  [Fic]—dc21

                                              2003005213

                    10 9 8 7 6 5 4 3 2 1

            Proprietary ISBN 978-1-101-95132-3
          Part of Boxed Set, ISBN 978-1-101-95128-6

Doggone It!

by Nancy Krulik • illustrated by John & Wendy

Grosset & Dunlap

Chapter 1

"Are they here yet?" Jeremy Fox asked, as he rode his bike up to Katie Carew's house early Saturday morning.

Katie was sitting on the front porch with her dog, Pepper. *Waiting.*

"Nope." Katie told her best friend. "And I've been sitting here all morning."

"You still don't know anything about the new neighbors?" Jeremy plopped down beside her. "I thought your parents met them already."

Katie shook her head. "My mom won't even give me a hint about what they're like. She thinks it's better if I'm surprised."

"That's *so* not fair," Jeremy said.

"I hope they have a lot of kids," Katie thought out loud.

Just then, Katie's other best friend, Suzanne Lock, came skipping rope around the corner. As she reached Katie's house, Suzanne put down her jump rope and glared at Jeremy. "What are you doing here?" she demanded.

"Waiting for Katie's new neighbors."

Suzanne turned to Katie. "I thought *we* were going to meet your new neighbors together."

"We are," Katie assured her other best friend. "Jeremy wants to see them, too."

"Three's a crowd," Suzanne complained.

"So leave," Jeremy told her.

Katie shook her head. She liked both of her best friends so much. It was too bad they couldn't like each other. "Come on, you guys," she said. "This is a really important day. There's a new family moving in next door."

"I hope they have a teenage girl," Suzanne told Katie. "Then we can find out about the newest music and clothes before anyone else. Teenagers know all about that kind of stuff."

Jeremy scowled. "Who needs another teenage girl around here? I'd rather have a couple of new boys in the neighborhood." He stopped and thought for a moment. "Maybe they'll put up a basketball hoop over their garage."

"Girls play basketball, too," Katie reminded him.

"Yeah," Suzanne added. "Ever hear of the WNBA?"

"You're right," Jeremy admitted. "But we just got a new girl in the neighborhood."

"You mean Becky?" Katie asked him. Becky Stern had moved to Cherrydale from Atlanta about two months ago. But she already had so many friends that it was weird to think of her as the "new girl."

"Becky, your *girlfriend*," Suzanne added with a giggle.

Jeremy turned beet red. "She is *not* my girlfriend," he insisted. "Take that back."

But Suzanne wouldn't give in. "Jeremy and

Becky sitting in a tree, K-I-S-S-I-N-G," she sang. "First comes love. Then comes marriage. Then comes little Jeremy in a baby carriage. Sucking his thumb, wetting his pants, doing the hootchie-cootchie dance!"

Now Jeremy was really mad. "She is *not* my girlfriend," he insisted.

"She wishes she was," Suzanne told him. "Everyone knows it."

"That's not my problem," Jeremy said. He blushed again.

"I wonder if the new family will have a dog," Katie said, quickly changing the subject. "Pepper would like that."

"*Arf!*" At the sound of his name, the chocolate-and-white cocker spaniel looked up at Katie and smiled.

"See?" Katie asked. She kissed her dog on the head. "He'd love a four-legged friend."

"Yeah, but what if the new family has a cat?" Suzanne asked. "That wouldn't be so great."

"Why not? Pepper can be friends with a cat."

Jeremy shook his head at that. "A cat and a dog? I don't know, Katie."

"Pepper's not like other dogs," Katie insisted. "He's special."

Before anyone could argue with that, a huge white moving van came rumbling down the street.

"They're here!" Katie yelled excitedly.

Suzanne stood up and fixed her hair. "How do I look?" she asked.

The kids all watched as two big men got out of the van and began to unload the new neighbors' belongings. Before long there were chairs, tables, lamps, and a big wooden bed on the front lawn.

"I don't see any toys," Katie said nervously.

"They're probably packed away in boxes," Jeremy reasoned.

Just then, a red car pulled into the driveway beside the house.

"That's the new family!" Katie cheered. "Let's go meet them." She started to run over toward the car.

Katie didn't get very far. She stopped dead in her tracks and stared, as a woman with dark, short hair and small, round glasses got out of the car. She looked really familiar.

Frighteningly familiar!

"It can't be . . ." Suzanne began.

"I think it is," Jeremy told her. He looked again. "Oh yeah. It's her, all right."

"Oh no!" Katie cried out. "This is awful!"

Chapter 2

There was no doubt about it. The woman who had gotten out of the car was Mrs. Derkman, Katie's third-grade teacher—*strict* Mrs. Derkman, the teacher with the most rules in the whole school.

"Suzanne, can you believe how horrible this is?" Katie exclaimed.

Suzanne didn't answer. She just stood there with her mouth wide open as Mrs. Derkman walked toward the kids.

"*You* bought the house next to mine?" Katie asked in disbelief.

"Didn't your mother tell you?" Mrs. Derkman replied.

"I um . . . she . . . I think she wanted it to be a surprise," Katie stammered.

"And we are *definitely* surprised!" Jeremy said.

"I can tell." Mrs. Derkman laughed. "Suzanne, please close your mouth before a bug flies down your throat."

"Barbara, which of these boxes goes in the bathroom?" Mr. Derkman called to his wife.

Barbara? Katie had never thought of Mrs. Derkman as someone with a first name before.

"Well, I'd better get to work. I have a whole house to unpack." Mrs. Derkman smiled at Katie. "We'll talk later, *neighbor*."

"Yes, Mrs. Derkman," Katie answered quietly.

As Mrs. Derkman headed toward her new house, Jeremy strapped on his helmet and walked over to his bike.

"I . . . well . . . I gotta get home," he said nervously.

"Don't you want to play ball or something?" Katie asked him.

Jeremy looked at Mrs. Derkman and her husband. They were on their front porch, watching the movers. "Not today, Katie," Jeremy told her. "Maybe we can play tomorrow . . . at *my* house."

As Jeremy rode off, Katie smiled at Suzanne. "I'll go get my jump rope. We can make up some new rhymes or something."

Suzanne picked up her rope. "Uh, I have to be getting home," she told Katie nervously.

"It's getting late."

Katie looked at her friend. "Late for what?"

"Um, um . . . I just have to go," Suzanne said.

Katie looked down at Pepper. "At least *you* still want to play with me, don't you, boy?" she asked, scratching the spaniel between the ears.

Crash! One of the movers dropped a heavy box on the lawn. The loud noise scared Pepper. He turned and ran inside as fast he could.

Next door, Mrs. Derkman was yelling at the movers. She sounded angry and impatient— just the way she did when the kids in class 3A wouldn't listen.

"This is a nightmare!" Katie exclaimed.

Chapter 3

"Would you like some more carrots?"
Katie's mother asked at dinner that night.

"No thanks," Katie mumbled.

"But you've hardly eaten a thing," Mrs.
Carew said. "I made all your favorites—veggie
burgers, carrots, and mashed potatoes."

Katie sighed. Veggie burgers were her
favorite. But she didn't feel much like eating.

"I'm not hungry," she mumbled.

"Well, I'll have some more carrots—and
potatoes, too," Katie's dad said, patting his
stomach. "This is a great dinner."

Katie's mother smiled. "Speaking of
dinner, I was thinking we should invite the

Derkmans for a barbecue tomorrow. They've probably been too busy unpacking to cook."

Katie gulped. Mrs. Derkman? Eating at her house? How horrible was that?

"No!" Katie shouted out suddenly.

Her mother looked surprised. "What do you mean 'no'?"

Katie sighed. Didn't her mother understand *anything?* "Mom, Mrs. Derkman is my teacher. I can't have dinner with her."

"Katie, that's silly. The Derkmans just moved in. We should be neighborly," her mother said firmly.

"There are a gazillion houses." Katie moaned. "Why did they have to pick the one right next door to us? I wish . . ."

Katie was about to say that she wished anyone else in the whole world had moved in next door, but she stopped herself. Katie knew better than to make wishes like that. It was too dangerous.

Katie had learned all about wishes after one really bad day at school. She'd lost thefootball game for her team, ruined her favorite jeans, and burped in front of the whole class. That day, Katie had wished that she could be anyone but herself.

There must have been a shooting star flying overhead or something when she made that wish, because the very next day the magic wind came.

The magic wind was a really wild storm that seemed to blow only around Katie. The magic wind was really powerful. So powerful, in fact, that it was able to turn Katie into somebody else.

The first time the magic wind came, it changed Katie into Speedy, the class hamster.

She'd spent a whole morning running around trying to keep from getting stepped on.

Luckily, Katie had changed back into herself before anyone realized who the class hamster really was.

The magic wind didn't only turn Katie into animals. Sometimes it turned her into grown-ups, like Lucille, the school lunch lady, and Mr. Kane, the principal.

Other times, the magic wind turned Katie into other kids, like Suzanne's baby sister, Heather, or Becky Stern, the new girl in school. Once it had actually switcherooed her into Jeremy Fox. Katie didn't like being a boy at all. She wasn't even sure which bathroom she was supposed to go into!

That's why Katie didn't make wishes anymore. When they came true, things never turned out the way she hoped they would. The truth was, Mrs. Derkman was her neighbor, and there was nothing Katie could do.

But that didn't mean she had to like it.

Chapter 4

Slurp. Katie was fast asleep when she felt a wet lick on her face. She opened her eyes slowly and came face-to-face with Pepper. As soon as Katie opened her eyes, the spaniel's brown stubby tail began wagging wildly.

Katie glanced at the clock on her wall. It was only 7:15. "Didn't anybody tell you it's Sunday?" she moaned to her dog.

Pepper answered with a big, soggy lick to her nose.

"Okay, okay," she giggled. "You win. Let's go play."

Just then, Katie heard someone singing loudly outside. Whoever it was had a terrible

voice—high and screechy, like fingernails on a blackboard.

Pepper growled.

"Who could that be?" Katie wondered aloud as she put on her clothes. Quickly, she brushed her teeth and raced outside to find out what was going on.

Whoa! What a surprise!

When Katie and Pepper walked out into Katie's front yard, they discovered Mrs. Derkman working in her garden. The teacher was wearing a huge straw hat and a pair of overalls. Her hands were covered with green gardening gloves. And as if that weren't weird enough . . .

Mrs. Derkman was singing at the top of her lungs.

"Noah, he built them, he built them an arky-arky," the teacher screeched.

Katie couldn't believe that this was the same Mrs. Derkman who was her teacher. Mrs. Derkman never wore anything other

than neat dresses and sensible shoes. And she never—*ever*— sang out loud.

"Made it out of hickory barky-barky . . ." Mrs. Derkman croaked.

Katie choked back a laugh.

"*Ruff! Ruff!*" Pepper came racing over to Katie with a yellow tennis ball in his mouth. He wanted to play.

"Okay, boy," Katie said with a smile. She took the soggy ball and flung it across the lawn. "Fetch!"

Unfortunately, Katie's aim wasn't very good. The ball flew into Mrs. Derkman's garden. Pepper leaped right into the flowerbed and caught the ball in his mouth.

"Oh, no! Not my pansies!" Mrs. Derkman waved her arms wildly. "Get out of here, you rotten dog!"

Pepper cocked his head curiously to the side. He'd just caught the ball in the air. Usually somebody said "good dog" after he did that. Sometimes he even got a treat.

But Mrs. Derkman certainly wasn't about to give Pepper a treat.

Katie walked over to Mrs. Derkman's house. "Sorry about that," she said shyly.

"My new flowerbed." Mrs. Derkman moaned. "Katie, could you please keep this dog on your lawn from now on?"

"His name is Pepper," Katie told her.

Mrs. Derkman took a deep breath. "Okay, could you please keep Pepper on your lawn?"

Katie nodded. "I'm sorry about your flowers."

"It's okay," Mrs. Derkman said. "Just please keep *Pepper* out of my garden. I've planted a new strawberry patch and some tomato plants. They have to be treated very tenderly. Don't they, Sven?"

Sven? Katie looked around. "Who are you talking to?" she asked her teacher curiously.

Mrs. Derkman laughed. "Sven," she said, pointing to the big stone troll standing in the middle of the garden. "We've had him for years. I found him when I was visiting

Norway, and I just fell in love with him."

Katie looked at the troll. It had a pointy red hat and a creepy smile on its face. It definitely wasn't loveable!

"I talk to Sven all the time," Mrs. Derkman continued. "It's a kind of game I play to pass the time while I'm working in the garden."

How weird is that? Katie wondered to herself.

"I love gardening!" Mrs. Derkman told Katie. "I spend every hour I can out here with my little babies." Mrs. Derkman ran her hand lovingly over one of her pansies.

"It seems like a lot of work," Katie said.

Mrs. Derkman nodded. "It is. But I don't mind. My plants are worth it. I water them and fertilize them. They especially love when I sing to them."

For a minute, Katie thought her teacher was going to burst into song once again. Luckily, at just that second, Mr. Derkman came out onto the porch. He was wearing a

red flannel bathrobe. His long, hairy legs stuck out from under the robe.

"Hi, Katie," Mr. Derkman said, waving. He looked down at Pepper. "Cute dog. He's a cocker spaniel right?"

Katie nodded.

"I had a beagle when I was growing up," Mr. Derkman recalled. "Barbara, isn't it wonderful to have a cute dog living right next door?"

Mrs. Derkman rolled her eyes. "Wonderful," she said sarcastically.

Mr. Derkman held out a big mug. "Snookums, your coffee is ready," he told his wife.

Mrs. Derkman stood and wiped some dirt from her overalls. "Okay, Freddy Bear," she said. "I'll be right in."

Snookums? Freddy Bear? Katie couldn't wait to tell the kids at school about this!

On second thought, they'd probably never believe her.

Chapter 5

The moment Katie walked onto the playground on Monday morning, she was surrounded by the other kids from class 3A.

"Suzanne told us Mrs. Derkman moved in next door to you," Zoe Canter said. "Is it true?"

Katie nodded.

"I told you so," Suzanne told the kids. "I was right there with her when Mrs. Derkman drove up."

"Hey, I was there, too," Jeremy announced. "I was there *first*."

"Jeremy you're such a good friend," Becky Stern said. She smiled brightly at him.

Jeremy blushed.

"Oh, Katie!" Miriam Chan exclaimed. "I'm so sorry."

"What's it like living next door to a teacher?" Becky asked.

"It's awful," Suzanne butted in. "Isn't it, Katie?"

"It's definitely horrible," Katie agreed. "I

mean, last night, Mrs. Derkman and her husband came over for a barbecue. How embarrassing is that?"

"Mrs. Derkman came to your house?" Kevin Camilleri asked with surprise.

Katie nodded. "Mr. Derkman brought his ukulele. He played songs, and Mrs. Derkman danced."

Jeremy's eyes opened wide. "Mrs. Derkman *danced?*"

Katie nodded. "You should have seen her. She was doing a Hawaiian hula."

The kids all tried to picture their teacher wiggling her hips in Katie's backyard. But they couldn't. It was too weird to even imagine.

"You had to be there," Katie told them. "It was gross. But not as gross as the strawberry pie she baked. That was all burnt."

"I can't eat strawberries," Mandy Banks said. "I'm allergic to them."

"I'm allergic to *Mrs. Derkman*. I feel so bad

for you, Katie Kazoo," George Brennan said, using the special nickname he'd made up for Katie.

George and Mrs. Derkman did not get along well at all. George told a lot of jokes. Mrs. Derkman didn't like any kidding around in her classroom. "I knew you would understand how I feel," Katie said. "You'd definitely hate living next door to Mrs. Derkman."

"I hate living on the same *planet* as Mrs. Derkman," George agreed.

Katie looked at Kevin. "It wouldn't be so bad for you, though, Kevin," Katie told him. "She's got tomato plants in her garden."

Kevin couldn't believe it. His teacher was growing his favorite food in her garden. "Do you think she'll bring tomatoes to school?" he asked.

"I wouldn't eat them, Kev," George said. "What if she's like that witch in *Snow White?* One bite of a Derkman tomato and you'll

sleep until a girl kisses you." George pretended to faint.

"You guys should see this garden," Katie continued. "It's huge. And in the middle, she has this ugly troll statue—that she *talks* to! It's the creepiest thing I ever saw."

"Mrs. Derkman is the creepiest thing *I* ever saw," George joked.

"Do you think Mrs. Derkman will treat you special now that she's your neighbor?" Zoe asked Katie. "Maybe she'll give you less homework or let you go to the bathroom whenever you want."

"I don't know," Katie said. "Do you think she'd do that?"

"It would be the *least* she could do," Suzanne assured her.

Hmmm. Katie smiled. Maybe there was a bright side to this whole mess after all.

Chapter 6

Or maybe there wasn't a bright side.

"What good is it having a teacher live next door if she's still mean?" Katie exclaimed that night, as she and her parents sat together in the living room. "I think she was stricter with me today than she was with anyone else."

Mrs. Carew put her arm around her daughter. "I know it's kind of strange having her as your neighbor. But I'm sure she isn't treating you any worse because of it."

"Yes, she is," Katie insisted. "Today she called on me when she was sure I didn't know the answer. And she wouldn't let me go to the bathroom until Suzanne came back."

"But Mrs. Derkman always does things like that," Mrs. Carew said. "She hasn't changed
at all."

Katie frowned.

Mr. Carew reached into his pocket and pulled out a small, white envelope. "Speaking of Mrs. Derkman, I found this in the mailbox today. It's from her."

Katie gulped. A note from her teacher! This could be really bad.

"What does it say?" Katie's mom asked.

"Dear Mr. and Mrs. Carew," Katie's dad read out loud. "I am writing to tell you that your dog ate all the strawberries from my plants. From now on, please keep your dog on a leash. If you insist on letting him run wild, I will have to call the authorities. Sincerely, Barbara Derkman."

Now Katie was really mad. "Pepper would never eat her strawberries," she insisted.

"I know," Katie's dad agreed. "But some

dog must have."

"Then put *that* dog on a leash," Katie said.

Mrs. Carew put her arm around Katie.
"We'll put Pepper on a leash for a few days.

Then, when Mrs. Derkman finds out who's really eating her strawberries, things can go back to normal."

"But Pepper's lived here for years. He's hardly ever been on a leash, and he's never caused any trouble." Katie thought for a minute. "In fact, there weren't any problems in this neighborhood before Mrs. Derkman moved here. Maybe *she's* the one who needs to be walked on a leash!"

"Katie, I'm sorry, but Pepper's going to have to be on a leash for a while. Just until we can clear his good name," Mrs. Carew said.

"It won't be so bad," Katie's dad added. "We'll get Pepper one of those leashes with plastic jewels on it. He'll feel like a movie star."

Katie looked lovingly at Pepper. He was a good dog. All the kids liked him. That was more than she could say about Mrs. Derkman.

It just wasn't fair.

Chapter 7

The next day, Suzanne, Jeremy, Becky, and George walked Katie home from school. They were trying to cheer her up. But nothing they said or did could make Katie feel better.

She would never feel better again. At least, not as long as Mrs. Derkman was around.

Luckily, when the kids reached Katie's house, Mrs. Derkman *wasn't* around. Her car wasn't in the driveway, and the lights were all off inside the house.

"Hey, she's not here!" Katie exclaimed. "You guys want to stay for a while? Maybe play tag or something?"

"Well, as long as Mrs. *Jerk*man's not

around . . ." George began.

That was all Jeremy needed to hear. "Tag! You're it!" he shouted, as he tapped George on the shoulder.

George didn't try racing back after Jeremy. It would be easier to tag Katie.

"Watch out, Katie Kazoo!" George shouted across the lawn. "Here I come!"

Katie took off like a rocket, trying to dodge George's outstretched arm. She smiled as she soared across her front lawn. Tag was Katie's favorite game.

But as she looked up toward her house, Katie's smile turned to a frown. She could see Pepper sitting in the front hall. His little

brown-and-white face was pressed up against the screen door.

Usually Pepper played tag, too. He would run on the lawn with the kids, barking happily and wagging his tail.

But that was before Mrs. Derkman moved in next door.

"Gotcha!" George shouted, tagging Katie on the shoulder. "Boy, you're easy, Katie Kazoo!"

Katie sighed. She wasn't *always* that easy to catch. She just hadn't been paying attention.

She was now. "Better run, George!" she said. "I'm going to tag you back!"

"Oh, come on." George moaned. "Everyone always gets me. You haven't tagged Suzanne or Becky yet."

Katie darted off in search of Suzanne. But before she could reach her friend, a familiar, angry voice rang out from the sidewalk.

"Katie! Be careful. You almost stepped on

my petunias!" Mrs. Derkman, shouted as she zoomed down the block on a shiny silver scooter. The teacher stopped right in front of Katie's house and took off her yellow-and-pink helmet.

The kids all stared at her. They'd never

seen their teacher on a scooter before.

"I hope you've all finished your math homework," Mrs. Derkman added strictly.

Jeremy, Suzanne, Becky, and George looked at each other nervously. Finished? They hadn't even *started* their math homework.

"I gotta go," George said suddenly.

"Me, too," Jeremy agreed. "I'll see you tomorrow, Katie." He ran off after George.

"Wait up, Jeremy," Becky called out in her thick southern accent. "I'm going your way." She ran off after him.

"I guess I have to go do my homework, too," Suzanne said.

Katie frowned. "Mrs. Derkman is ruining my life!"

Suzanne nodded. "I know. She's really mean." Suzanne looked over at Mrs. Derkman's house. The teacher was standing on the porch, watching the girls. "I wish I could stay and keep you company, but I really

gotta go." Suzanne said.

Katie shrugged. "It's okay. I have to take Pepper for his walk, anyhow."

"How's that leash thing going?"

"Lousy," Katie said. "Pepper hates it. My mom says he'll get used to it, but I don't think so."

As Suzanne walked away, Katie went inside to get Pepper's leash. She hooked it onto his collar and led him outside.

Katie was careful not to walk Pepper anywhere near Mrs. Derkman's lawn. The teacher had gone inside, but you never knew. Maybe she was spying on Katie through a window or something.

"I'm really sorry, Pepper," she said as led him down the block.

Pepper looked up at Katie with sad, brown eyes. He let out a little whimper. It was the only sound on the whole block. There was no one else around. Mrs. Derkman had made sure of that.

Katie didn't blame her friends for not wanting to play at her house. She didn't even like playing there anymore.

Katie sat down at the curb and petted Pepper's sad little head. Pepper reached up and gently licked her face. He knew it wasn't her fault.

Just then a cool breeze brushed against the back of Katie's neck. It started out gentle

enough, but within seconds, the breeze turned into a strong wind—a wind that was blowing only around Katie.

The magic wind was back!

As the wild tornado swirled faster and faster, Katie let go of Pepper's leash. She didn't want him to get stuck in her own private storm. "Run, Pepper, run!" she shouted, as the wind blew stronger and stronger.

And then, suddenly, it stopped. Just like that.

Slowly Katie opened her eyes. She looked around. Everything was sort of gray and dull.

Frantically, she searched for Pepper. She didn't see the cocker spaniel anywhere.

Katie gulped nervously. Had he gotten out of the way in time? Or had the magic wind blown him far from home?

Katie sniffed the ground beside her. Oh, good. She could smell Pepper nearby. He was safe.

Katie sniffed again. This time, Pepper's scent mixed in the air with the smell of a barbecue being lit. Someone was grilling hamburgers.

Yum! They smelled delicious.

Wait a minute. I don't eat hamburgers, Katie thought to herself. *I'm a vegetarian.*

Still, those burgers sure did smell good. Katie just had to have one. Quickly, she scampered off in the direction of the barbecue. As she ran, her stubby brown tail wagged wildly.

Her *tail?*

Oh no! Katie had turned into a dog.

Katie looked at her body. She was chocolate brown and white. The fur on her paws was soft and curly. And her long ears waved back and forth as she turned her head.

Katie hadn't turned into just any dog—she'd turned into Pepper!

Chapter 8

Katie sat back on her hind legs and looked at the world through Pepper's eyes. Everything seemed yellow, blue, and gray. Katie knew the stop sign on the corner should be red, but to her it looked pale yellow. The sign was sort of blurry, too. It was hard to see something so far away.

Katie was frightened. She really wanted to go home, run into her room, and hide under her bed until the magic wind came and changed her back.

Katie looked out in front of her. It was strange being so low to the ground. All she saw were the bottoms of things—tree trunks,

sign posts, and . . . *a fire hydrant.*

For some reason, the sight of the hydrant made Katie's tail wag wildly. She scampered over as quickly as she could and began to sniff.

Lots of dogs had been there before her. And every one of them had peed on the hydrant. Their stinky smells were everywhere.

Yuck! Katie thought to herself. But she couldn't stop herself from smelling. It was a dog thing.

Sniff, sniff. A big dog had visited the hydrant. Probably a German Shepherd.

Sniff, sniff. There'd been a little dog there as well. *Really* little, like a Chihuahua or something.

Katie wanted to leave her mark, too. She picked up her hind leg and left a puddle. Then she dug wildly at the dirt under her feet. There. Now all the other dogs would know she'd been there.

When she was through peeing and digging, Katie decided to head for home. She didn't get very far, however, before a sweet, fruity smell reached her nose. There, in the middle of the sidewalk, was a half-chewed blueberry bagel.

Mmmm. People food.

I shouldn't eat that, Katie told herself. Who knows where its been. She sniffed at the bagel. It smelled so good, she couldn't help herself.

Crunch. She snatched up the treat and started to chew.

This is so gross, Katie thought, as bits of sidewalk sand and dirt scratched against her

tongue. But she didn't spit the bagel out. It tasted too good.

Katie's stubby little tail wagged happily back and forth as she ate. "I wonder if I can catch that?" she barked to herself as she swallowed the last bit of dirty bagel.

Katie turned toward her tail and stretched her neck back. Her tail was still very far away. She reached farther back. She began turning around and around in a circle, as she tried to grab her tail.

Whooaa, I'm getting dizzy, Katie thought as she spun.

Still, she didn't stop. She was determined to chase her tail—although she wasn't quite sure what she would do with it if she caught it.

Boy, dogs sure do weird things, she thought.

Just then, Katie heard a squeaky chattering noise. She sat still and quietly.

The noise seemed to be coming from a

nearby oak tree. Katie put her nose to the ground and sniffed. Her tail began to wag wildly.

Oh boy! *SQUIRREL*!

Katie darted off toward the oak tree. But the squirrel was quicker. He scrambled up the tree trunk.

The squirrel was high in the tree—too high for Katie to ever reach him. But that didn't stop her from trying. She leaped up and down at the base of the tree, barking wildly.

The squirrel sat on its high branch, chattering away. That rotten rodent was laughing at Katie.

Plink. An acorn landed on Katie's nose. The squirrel laughed harder.

Now Katie was really mad. She jumped higher. She barked louder.

The squirrel just kept on laughing.

Finally, Katie gave up. She wasn't going to catch the squirrel . . . at least not now.

I'll be back! Katie gave one last bark and started for home.

Just as Katie reached her front porch, she heard a loud, high-pitched dog yelp. It was coming from Mrs. Derkman's yard.

From the sound of the bark, Katie could tell this was a really small dog. But that didn't mean anything. Even small dogs could be mean. They had sharp teeth, and they weren't afraid to use them—especially if they thought a bigger dog was in their territory.

Katie sat still, watching.

Chapter 9

Katie's brown-and-white doggie eyes grew large as she watched with surprise at what happened next.

The little white dog took a big bite of one Mrs. Derkman's cucumbers! The white dog was the mysterious fruit and vegetable thief!

Unfortunately, Mrs. Derkman didn't know about the white dog. She was sure to blame the missing cucumber on Pepper. She was going to say he'd been running loose again.

Which he was . . . sort of. But it wasn't Katie's fault. It was the magic wind's fault.

There was no way Katie could explain that to Mrs. Derkman. The teacher would never

believe that Katie had actually turned into her own dog!

"*Grrrr!*" Katie let out a loud, frustrated growl.

The scraggly pup looked up in fear. Her ears stood straight up on her head. She sniffed around nervously. Then she began to whimper.

Oh no! Katie had made the puppy cry.

"Calm down, little puppy," Katie whispered softly.

But the puppy kept crying.

Katie had to let the white dog know that she wanted to be friends. She padded over and gave the pup a real doggie greeting: she sniffed at the dog's rear end. That was the way dogs said "hello."

The puppy's tail began to wag happily. Katie sniffed again. *Pew.* The dog's bottom smelled awful.

"I'm glad people don't say hello this way," Katie told herself as she sniffed even harder. "It's gross!"

The puppy was so happy to have a friend. She jumped up and let out a little squeal of joy. Then she turned around and nipped at Katie's nose. Lucky for Katie, the dog still had her puppy teeth.

Katie wondered where this scraggly white dog had come from. She didn't have a collar or tags. She was very skinny, and she smelled like she'd never had a bath in her whole life.

Katie didn't have a lot of time to feel bad for the puppy. Suddenly, she heard chattering

noises coming from a nearby tree.

Katie would know that sound anywhere—the squirrel was back!

This time, she was going to get that furry-tailed acorn thrower!

Without thinking, Katie took off after the squirrel. She kept her eyes on him the whole time—which is why she didn't notice the statue in the middle of the garden.

Bam! Katie ran right into Mrs. Derkman's beloved troll. The troll fell backward and bashed its head on a rock. The top of its pointy red hat crumbled into a thousand pieces.

As if that weren't bad enough, the squirrel got away. It was sitting on a high branch, laughing. Katie leaped up on the tree and barked wildly.

Katie's angry shouts scared the little puppy. She let out a big yelp and raced off.

"Come back!" Katie barked to the dog. "I can help you!"

The scrawny white pup didn't seem to hear Katie barking. But Mrs. Derkman did. She came running to find out what the all the noise was about.

Mrs. Derkman didn't see the little puppy that had been eating her cucumbers. She didn't see the squirrel laughing in the tree.

All the teacher saw was Pepper sitting in the middle of her tomato plants.

"Get out of here, you trouble-making dog!" she shouted.

Katie didn't have to be told twice. She ran off as fast as her four legs could carry her.

Chapter 10

Katie sat, huddled against the side of her house. Her little brown-and-white body shook with fear. She whimpered sadly.

Pepper was in really big trouble. And it was all Katie's fault.

Katie recognized the sound of Mrs. Derkman's footsteps as the teacher raced up the front steps of the Carew house. "I've had it with that mutt," Mrs. Derkman muttered angrily to herself.

Katie listened as her mother opened the door of their house. "Mrs. Derkman, what a nice surprise," she heard her mother say.

"Well, you're half right," Mrs. Derkman

answered. "There have been a few surprises today. But none of them have been nice."

Katie gulped.

Unfortunately, Katie didn't get to hear any more of the conversation. The sudden whistling of strong winds blocked out any other sounds.

Wow. It felt like there was a real storm coming.

Katie looked around nervously. The leaves on the trees were still. The clouds in the sky didn't seem to be moving, either. The wild winds were only blowing around Katie.

The magic wind was back!

As the gusts swirled around her, Katie began to howl in fear. The tornado-like winds

were very strong, and she was very small. What if the winds picked her up and carried her someplace far away? Would she ever be able to find her way home?

Katie curled her body into a frightened ball. She covered her eyes with her front paws and waited.

There was nothing else she could do. She couldn't stop the magic wind. It had to stop itself.

And that's exactly what happened. The magic wind stopped blowing, just as suddenly as it had begun. Katie slowly lifted her hands from her eyes. She looked around. Everything seemed clear and bright.

She stared down at her feet. There were her red sneakers. *Stop-sign* red.

She stared at her arms. There were five fingers on each hand . . . and no sign of fur anywhere.

Katie Kazoo was back!

So was Pepper. The cocker spaniel rubbed his furry body against Katie's legs.

"I'm so sorry, Pepper," Katie said. "I didn't mean to get you in trouble." She took Pepper's leash and slowly began to lead him toward her front porch.

Mrs. Derkman was just leaving. As she spotted Katie and Pepper, the teacher's mouth twisted into a tight frown. Her eyes bugged. Her cheeks turned red. She looked as though her head might explode!

Katie was sure Mrs. Derkman was going to scream at her. But the teacher didn't say a word. She just stormed back home.

Chapter 11

"It's just awful, Suzanne," Katie said into the phone later that night. "Mrs. Derkman was yelling at my mom."

"Mrs. Derkman shouts all the time," Suzanne reminded her. "Ask George. She's *always* yelling at him."

"But not like this," Katie explained. "She said if she ever caught Pepper on her lawn again, she would call the dog catcher!"

"Wow," Suzanne said. "That *is* really bad."

"I know," Katie agreed. "Mrs. Derkman told my mother to build a fence around our yard. That way, she could be sure Pepper would never get into her garden again."

"What did your mom say?"

"She told Mrs. Derkman we couldn't afford to do that," Katie said. "But Mrs. Derkman didn't care."

"So what are you going to do?" Suzanne asked. "Can you keep Pepper from eating her vegetables?"

Katie frowned. Even her best friend believed Pepper was the veggie thief. "It isn't Pepper."

Suzanne sighed. "Katie, I know you love Pepper and all, but maybe he *is* eating them.

You said Mrs. Derkman caught him right in the yard. And he did break her troll."

"That wasn't his fault," Katie said. "He was chasing this really mean squirrel."

Suzanne laughed. "Come on, Katie, are you saying it was the squirrel's fault?"

"Yes!" Katie exclaimed. "You don't know this squirrel. He's a tease. He laughs at Pepper and throws acorns at him, and . . ." Katie stopped in the middle of her sentence. She knew she was telling the truth.

She also knew Suzanne would never believe her.

"Anyway, Pepper isn't the one eating her vegetables," Katie continued. "It's this little white puppy. I saw her."

"Did someone on your block get a puppy?" Suzanne asked excitedly.

"No. I think she's a stray. And you can bet if Mrs. Derkman sees the puppy on her lawn, she's going to call the dog catcher."

"Oh, the poor puppy," Suzanne said.

"I'm telling you, Suzanne, I've never known anyone who hates dogs so much," Katie added.

"Mrs. Derkman hates all animals," Suzanne said. "She doesn't go near Speedy's cage since he got loose that time."

Katie giggled to herself. She knew all about that. After all, she'd *been* Speedy that morning. Katie would never forget the look of fear in Mrs. Derkman's eyes when she saw the class hamster running across the floor.

"I'll bet Mrs. Derkman never had a pet when she was growing up," Suzanne continued. "No one who ever had a pet could hate animals this much."

"Suzanne, you're a genius!" Katie exclaimed suddenly.

"I know," Suzanne agreed. Then she stopped for a minute. "*Why* am I genius?" she asked curiously.

"You've just solved Pepper's problem."

"I have?" Suzanne asked.

"Yes," Katie said. "But it's going to take a lot of work. Will you help me?"

"Sure," Suzanne agreed. "What do you want me to do?"

"The first thing you need to do is talk your mom into letting us use your basement for a few days." Katie told her. "We need to get started right away."

Chapter 12

"Hi, girls," Mrs. Carew said, as Katie and Suzanne ran into Katie's house after school the next day. "Do you want a snack?"

"No thanks, Mom. We've got too much to do," Katie answered.

Mrs. Carew shrugged. "Okay, I have some bills to pay anyway. I'll be in my room if you need me."

Katie waited until her mother was all the way upstairs before she started executing her plan.

"Get the peanut butter from the refrigerator, Suzanne?" Katie asked, finally.

"I thought we didn't have time for a

snack," Suzanne answered.

"It's not for us." Katie bent down and picked up one of Pepper's toy bones.

Pepper sat up tall, waiting. He thought Katie was going to play fetch with him.

No such luck.

"Sorry, boy," Katie told him. "I need to borrow this for someone else."

Katie covered both ends of the bone with peanut butter. Then she stuffed a few of Pepper's treats in her pocket. "Okay, let's go in the backyard," she told Suzanne.

"What are we going to do out there?" Suzanne asked.

Katie smiled. "You'll see."

Katie walked outside and placed the bone on the grass below her backyard deck. Then she walked back over to Suzanne, who was standing near the side of the house.

The girls stared at the bone. They waited.

And waited.

And waited some more.

"Nothing's happening," Suzanne complained.

"It will," Katie assured her. "That bone is perfect."

Suzanne looked curiously at her best friend. "I don't get it. How is a peanut-butter bone going to get Pepper out of trouble?"

Katie pointed to the bone. "That's how."

Suzanne looked where Katie was pointing. There, in the middle of Katie's lawn, sat the little white puppy. Her tail wagged excitedly as she licked the peanut butter from the bone.

"Who's that?" Suzanne asked.

"That's the vegetable thief," Katie answered. She reached into her pocket and pulled out a tasty dog treat.

The white puppy lifted her nose in the air and sniffed. As soon as she spotted Katie, she froze in place. She wasn't sure whether to grab

the treat or run away.

The puppy was very hungry, and the treat was very tempting. Finally, the dog scampered over toward Katie. She opened her mouth and snatched the treat from Katie's fingers.

Katie scooped the pup up in her arms and carried her over to the side of the house. "That's a good girl." Katie petted the dog's back gently. "Don't be scared. I want to help you."

The dog struggled for a moment. Katie gave her another treat. The pup calmed down and began to chew.

"Isn't she cute?" Katie asked Suzanne.

Suzanne stared at the scrawny puppy with the dirty, matted fur. She wrinkled up her nose. "That dog stinks."

"I know," Katie agreed. "But we're going to clean her up. And then we're going to teach her a few tricks. When we're finished, *no one* will be able to resist her."

Chapter 13

Katie and Suzanne kept the stray in Suzanne's basement. Mrs. Lock wasn't thrilled about having a dog in the house, but she agreed to let the puppy stay for a few days, if the girls promised to walk her and feed her, as long as Suzanne didn't get too attached to her.

"There's no way we can handle adopting a dog right now," Mrs. Lock told the girls. "I have enough to do with baby Heather."

"We're just watching her for a little while," Suzanne assured her mom.

The girls took good care of the little puppy. They bathed her in the basement sink

and made her a bed from a broken bread basket. They fed her and gave her plenty of water.

And every afternoon after school, they worked on training her.

Finally, after about a week, Katie and Suzanne were ready to give the puppy a test. They wanted to see how much she had learned.

Katie stood and looked firmly at the white puppy. "Sit," she said.

The puppy sat up tall.

Katie walked away. "Stay," she ordered.

The puppy stayed right where she was.

Katie sat down on her knees. "Come," she said.

The puppy scampered over to Katie.

"Good girl." Katie handed her a treat. "I think she's ready," she told Suzanne.

"Do you really think this is going to work?" Suzanne asked.

"It just has to," Katie answered.

Katie scooped up the puppy and began walking toward Mrs. Derkmans' house. When they reached their teacher's front door, Katie put the puppy on the porch.

"Stay," she said firmly. Then she rang the doorbell and ran away.

Katie went over to where Suzanne was hiding behind an old tree. Together, the girls watched as the Derkmans' door opened.

Mr. Derkman looked outside. At first he didn't see anyone. Then he noticed the small white puppy.

"Aren't you just the cutest little thing?" He lifted her into his arms. "Kootchy-kootchy-koo."

Katie smiled. At least *Mr.* Derkman liked the puppy.

"Freddy Bear, who is it?" Mrs. Derkman asked, as she came to the door. She saw the

dog in her husband's arms. "Oh, no. Where did that thing come from?"

"Someone left her on our doorstep."

"Well, get rid of it. Go call the animal shelter."

"But Snookums, look how cute she is," Mr. Derkman pleaded.

"I don't want to look at her. I want you to get rid of her," Mrs. Derkman insisted.

Katie gulped. Things were not going the way she'd planned. She'd thought her teacher would fall in love with the puppy at first sight. Katie figured that once Mrs. Derkman learned to love dogs, she'd be nicer to Pepper. But that wasn't what was happening at all. Mrs. Derkman hated the dog.

What a mess! First, Pepper had gotten in trouble, and now this poor little dog was going to be sent to a shelter—and it was all Katie's fault.

Suddenly, the puppy picked up her head and licked Mrs. Derkman on the hand.

"Yuck!" the teacher exclaimed. "Dog germs."

Mr. Derkman petted the puppy on the head. "I think she likes you, Snookums," he said.

"Don't be ridiculous," Mrs. Derkman said.

"She wants you to hold her," Mr. Derkman said. "Come on, just for a minute."

Mrs. Derkman sighed. "Fine. For a minute. Then you call the shelter."

Mr. Derkman placed the puppy in his wife's arms. The little dog snuggled up against Mrs. Derkman's shoulder.

The teacher slowly reached up and nervously stroked the puppy's fur. The puppy nuzzled closer against Mrs. Derkman's neck.

Mr. Derkman smiled. "She's awfully cute, Snookums. And she seems to need a home. We could give her a nice home."

Mrs. Derkman sighed. She'd seen that look in her husband's eyes before. There was no fighting him when he wanted something this badly.

"Well, I'm certainly not going to walk her," Mrs. Derkman told her husband.

"I'll do that," Mr. Derkman assured her.

"And I don't have time to brush her or bathe her," Mrs. Derkman continued.

"I'll take care of that," Mr. Derkman said. "I'll take care of everything. All you have to do is enjoy her."

Mrs. Derkman handed the dog over to her husband and shook her head. "That's going to be the hardest part," she said.

Chapter 14

A few mornings later, Katie awoke to a terrible screeching noise.

"How much is that doggie in the window?" Mrs. Derkman sang from her garden.

"Aroo!"

Mrs. Derkman and the dog were singing together! Katie had to see this! She dressed quickly, put Pepper on his leash, and headed outside.

Mrs. Derkman was working in her garden. The white puppy was sitting at her side. Neither the dog nor Mrs. Derkman seemed to notice Katie at first. They were too busy singing.

"There was a teacher, had a dog, and Snowball was her name-oh," Mrs. Derkman sang.

"*Ruff! Ruff!*" Snowball chimed in.

Mrs. Derkman stopped singing when she saw Katie and Pepper. "Hi, Katie," she said cheerfully.

"Hello," Katie said.

"Why don't you bring Pepper over here?" Mrs. Derkman said. "I'd like him to meet Snowball."

Katie was about to tell Mrs. Derkman that Pepper already knew Snowball, but she decided not to. It would be too hard to explain.

"You can take Pepper off the leash if you want," Mrs. Derkman said, as Katie led her dog into the teacher's yard.

Katie looked down as she unhooked Pepper's leash. She could see Snowball happily chomping on a cucumber. Mrs. Derkman didn't seem to mind at all.

"I suppose I owe you and Pepper an apology," Mrs. Derkman said slowly.

Katie didn't know what to say. She'd never heard her teacher apologize to anyone before.

The teacher watched as Pepper and Snowball sniffed each other. "I never dreamed it would be such fun to have a pet," she told Katie. "Snowball seems to like my singing even more than my plants do. And she's more

fun to talk to than Sven was."

Katie was amazed. Having a dog sure had changed Mrs. Derkman. She didn't seem as stern as she did in school.

"Now, don't you think you should go study for that Social Studies test?" Mrs. Derkman continued. "It's going to be very hard."

Okay, maybe she hadn't changed that much.

Katie watched as Pepper and Snowball barked at a squirrel in a tree. The squirrel didn't seem to like being outnumbered.

Katie smiled. It served him right.

"There was a teacher, had a dog, and Snowball was her name-oh," Mrs. Derkman began singing again.

"*Aroo!*" Snowball joined in with a loud howl.

Katie laughed. Having her teacher for a next-door neighbor wouldn't have been something Katie would have wished for. But maybe it wasn't going to be so bad after all.

Chapter 15

It didn't take long for Katie to teach Snowball a few simple tricks. You can teach your dog, too. All you have to do is follow these easy steps.

You will have to practice these tricks alot before your dog will learn them. Some dogs can learn tricks in a few days. It takes other dogs longer to learn.

Teach Your Dog to Sit: This is the easiest trick for your dog to learn. Start by holding a dog treat above her, just out of her reach. Your dog will look up. Then . . . whoops! She'll fall right into the sit position. As soon as your dog begins to fall back, say the word

"sit." Then be sure to give your dog a lot of praise—and the treat.

If you do this over and over, your dog will understand what the word "sit" means.

Teach Your Dog to Stay: Start by asking your dog to sit. Then hold your hand out so your palm is near her nose. This is your signal for "stay." Take a step backward, saying the word "stay." Before your dog can move toward you, hurry back to her. Give her a treat.

Repeat this a few times. Each time, move a little farther from your dog. Stay away from her for longer amounts of time, too. She'll soon learn to stay, no matter how far away you may seem.

* * *

Author's note: Katie was very lucky that Snowball was a sweet puppy. But there's no guarantee that other stray dogs are as nice. If you see a strange dog wandering your neighborhood, don't try to rescue her yourself. Instead, ask a grown-up to call a local shelter. They will send an expert to rescue the dog.

shows the Egyptian alphabet. Now she, Katie, and Suzanne can send notes to each other in ancient Egyptian.

That's going to make Mrs. Derkman really mad. After all, she doesn't have a copy of this chart.

But you do!

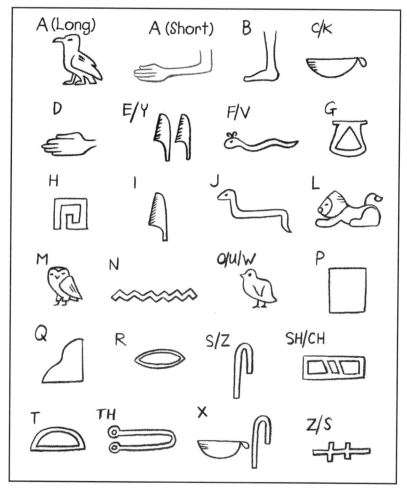